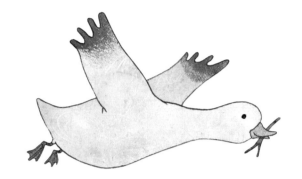

A Book of Babies

By Il Sung Na

ALFRED A. KNOPF

NEW YORK

When the flowers begin to bloom
and the world starts turning green,
animals everywhere are born . . .

. . . including the noisy ducklings.

S ome have lots of
brothers and sisters.

Some have none at all.

Some can walk right away,

While others need
a little help!

Some are carried in
their mommy's pouch.

Some are carried in their *daddy's* pouch!

Some are born with soft, warm fur,

While some are born with smooth scales.

B<small>UT</small> at the end of their very first day, babies everywhere need their rest . . .

. . . including the sleepy ducklings!

For all the mommies in the world

THIS IS A BORZOI BOOK PUBLISHED BY ALFRED A. KNOPF

Copyright © 2013 by Il Sung Na

All rights reserved. Published in the United States by Alfred A. Knopf, an imprint of
Random House Children's Books, a division of Random House, Inc., New York. Originally published
in slightly different form in Great Britain by Meadowside Children's Books, London, in 2013.

Knopf, Borzoi Books, and the colophon are registered trademarks of Random House, Inc.

Visit us on the Web! randomhouse.com/kids

Educators and librarians, for a variety of teaching tools, visit us at RHTeachersLibrarians.com

Library of Congress Cataloging-in-Publication Data
Na, Il Sung.
A book of babies / by Il Sung Na. — 1st American ed.
p.   cm.
Summary: While baby animals are born—some with fur and some with scales,
some with lots of brothers and sisters, some with none—a curious duck watches.
ISBN 978-0-385-75290-9 (trade) — ISBN 978-0-385-75291-6 (lib. bdg.) — ISBN 978-0-385-75292-3 (ebook)
1. Animals—Infancy—Juvenile fiction. [1. Animals—Infancy—Fiction. 2. Birth—Fiction. 3. Ducks—Fiction.] I. Title.
PZ10.3.N12Bm 2014
[E]—dc23
2012050490

The text of this book is set in 29-point Mrs Eaves.
The illustrations were created by combining handmade painterly textures
with digitally generated layers, which were then compiled in Adobe Photoshop.

MANUFACTURED IN CHINA
January 2014
10 9 8 7 6 5 4 3 2 1

First American Edition